Food +
Farming

Alfi Beasti, Don't Eat That!

✳ By Kate Hardy ✳

PUFFIN

Alfi Beasti was a fussy eater.
He ate everything he shouldn't
and nothing he should.

Mum's bags were always tasty...

"Alfi Beasti, don't eat that...

or that ..."

Alfi's mum had tried everything...

"Alfi Beasti,
why not try this?
It's tasty and healthy –
I'm sure you'll like fish!"

...but Alfi just wouldn't eat anything he was supposed to.

Then Alfi's mum and dad had an idea...

"We're taking you out for a treat today.
The posh shop in town has a new cafe.
Roasted slugs and porcupine tails,
pickled pigeon and purée of snails ...

soufflé of woodlice
and hot buttered mice ...

Try our
wonderful
NEW
Restaurant
on the
3rd floor

But Alfi didn't think it
sounded like a treat...

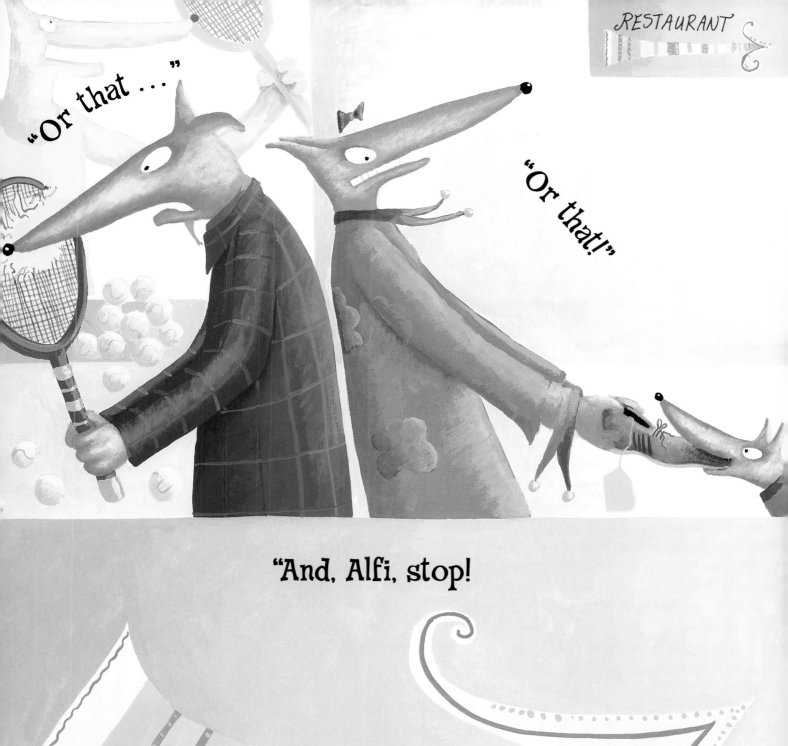

...HAT!"

Softbungelows Restaurant

Tasmanian Termite Soup
with a hint of fresh toad.
or
Pickled pigeon paté

Dish of the day:

Petrified partridge
on a sofa of pink cabbage

Desserts

Weasel feet cake
with fresh cat
cream
or
Kumquat Surp

Lunch was *not* a success.

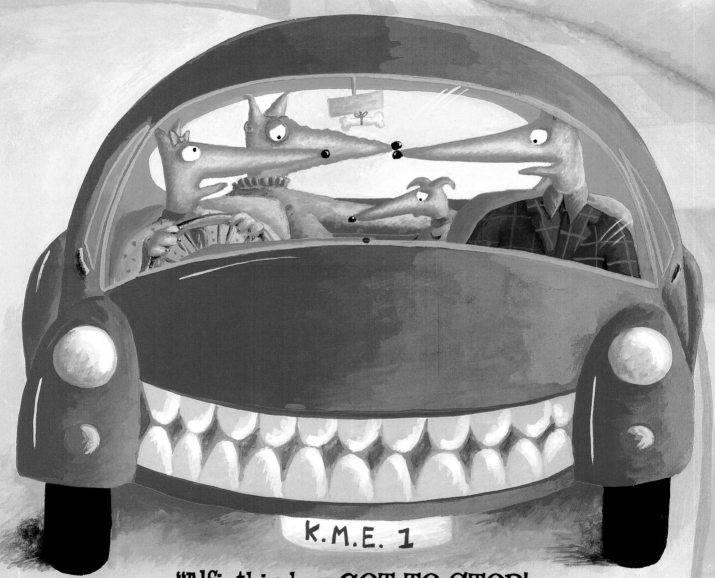

K.M.E. 1

"Alfi, this has GOT TO STOP!
You were supposed to eat lunch,
not the rest of that shop.
It's your birthday tomorrow; everyone's coming!
If we make a HUGE tea, will you PLEASE eat something?"

When at last it was Alfi's birthday, everyone was enjoying themselves so much they didn't notice how late it was...

"Look at the time – it's twelve o'clock. The house is a mess and we've still got to shop ..."

But Grandma's special presents
came to the rescue...

"Don't you worry
about the tea.
We can fix it,
Alfi and me."

So Alfi put on the new chef's outfit Grandma had bought him and they got to work in the kitchen.

"Stirring and mixing,
cooking and baking,
Alfi and Grandma are busily making...

"Try some broccoli trees and banana canoes, pizza fish and some toffee gnus ..."

"A spoonful of wobbly jelly cat and some incredible, edible birthday cake HAT!"

GRANDMA BEASTI'S RASPBERRY FLUFF PUDDING

The next day...

"Wow, what a party yesterday!
What a scrumptious yumptious sort of a day!
Alfi Beasti, your cooking was great,
you ate and you ate and you ate and you ATE!
But what about today?"

Well ... if you let
me help with every dish,
and we never again
have that scary fish.
Then ...

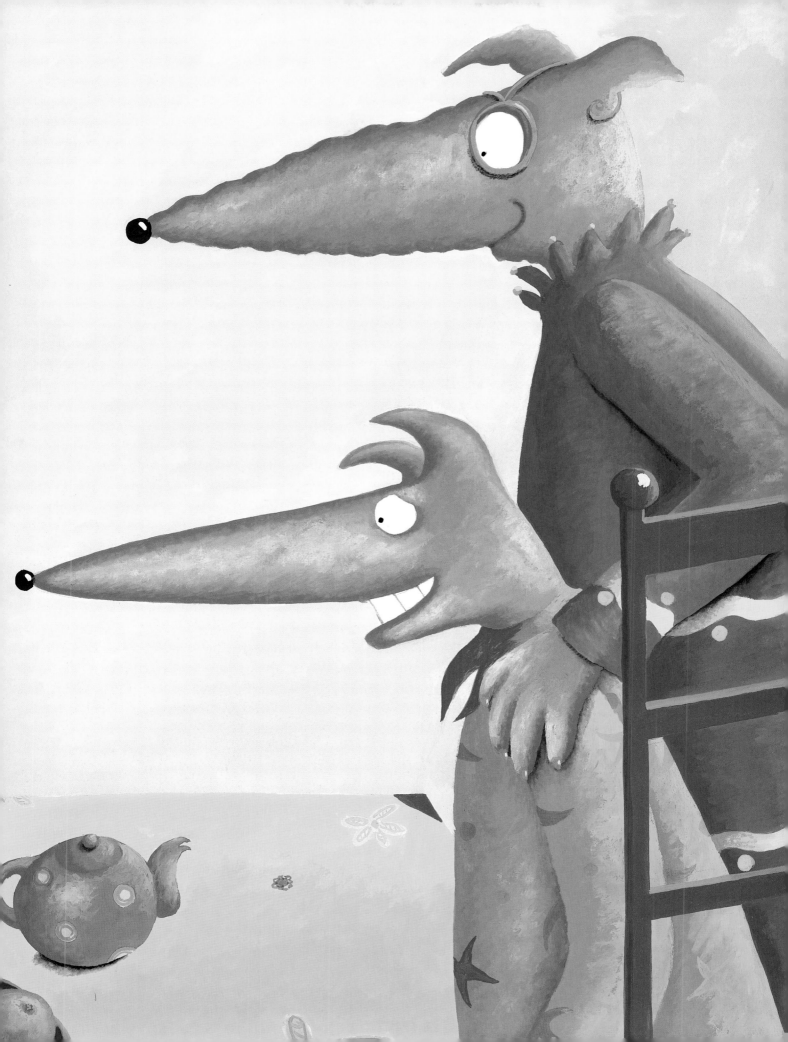

"Alfi Beasti does eat this ...

and this ...

"I still don't like sprouts, though!"

The End

 For Ezra, the olive-eater

PUFFIN BOOKS

Published by the Penguin Group: London, New York, Australia, Canada, India, New Zealand
and South Africa

Penguin Books Ltd, Registered Offices: 80 Strand, London WC2R ORL, England

www.penguin.com

First published in 2004

1 3 5 7 9 10 8 6 4 2

Copyright © Kate Hardy, 2004

Made and printed in China

ISBN 0-670-91301-4 Hardback

ISBN 0-140-56909-X Paperback